KU-167-727

A Templar Book

Produced by The Templar Company plc,
Pippbrook Mill, London Road, Dorking, Surrey RH4 1JE, Great Britain.

Text copyright © *The Fairy Kitten* 1926 by Darrell Waters Limited
Illustration and design copyright © 1995 by The Templar Company plc
Enid Blyton's signature mark is a registered trademark of Darrell Waters Limited

This edition produced for Parragon Books,
Unit 13-17, Avonbridge Trading Estate, Atlantic Road, Avonmouth, Bristol BS11 9QD

This book contains material first published as
The Fairy Kitten in Enid Blyton's Teacher's Treasury 1926.

Illustrated by Kate Davies

Printed and bound in Italy

ISBN 1-85813-623-7

POCKET LIBRARY

THE FAIRY KITTEN

Illustrated by Kate Davies

‖ •PARRAGON• ‖

There was once a little boy called John. He lived with his mother and father in a lovely little cottage at the edge of the woods. Usually he was a happy little boy, who laughed and played all day in the sunshine, but just lately he had been very unhappy because his little grey kitten had run away and got lost.

John had looked everywhere for
her – in the house, in the garden, in
the summer house, in the garage
and in the road.

"She may have run into the
wood," said his mother. "Go and
see if you can find her there, John."

So off John went to the woods
where primroses and celandines
were flowering, and where the
silver pussy willow shone pale and
soft in the warm spring sun.

But his kitten was nowhere to be found, and John could have cried with disappointment. He had so loved playing with her. He was sure he would never find another kitten that was as pretty as she was.

Suddenly he stopped still and listened. Was that a mew that he heard?

Surely it was!

The noise came again softly, very high and quiet, not exactly like a mew, but John couldn't think what else it could be. He began looking about to see where the noise came from. It sounded as though it came from somewhere low down.

Yes, it came from the middle of a prickly gorse bush! Surely his poor little kitty couldn't be in there!

"Kitty! Kitty!" he called, peeping into the bush.

A little high voice answered him.

"Oh, help me, please. I'm caught in the prickles!"

John was so surprised to hear the tiny voice, that he could hardly speak.

"Who are you?" he asked at last.

"I'm a pixie-piper," said the little voice. "The wind blew me right off my feet and landed me here, and I can't get out! Will you help me?"

"A pixie!" said John excitedly.

"Yes, I'll help you! I've never seen a pixie before! But, oh my! It's rather prickly!"

He put his hands right into the gorse bush and pressed back the branches. There, in the middle, was a tiny pixie, dressed in red and yellow. Carefully John lifted him out of the bush and set him down on the ground.

"Oh, thank you!" cried the pixie. "You are kind to help me, but look at your poor hands. They are covered in scratches and scrapes. And why do you look so unhappy?"

"I'm upset because I've lost my kitten," said John sadly, and told the little pixie all about it.

"Dear, dear, that's very sad!" said the piper. "But don't worry, I'll help you. I think I know where your kitten may be. The fairies love kittens. If they've found yours, they'll have changed her into a fairy kitten. She won't be very far away. But we will have to use some pixie magic to find her. Have you ever seen a fairy kitten?"

"No, but I'd *love* to," said John excitedly. "Where are they kept?"

"There's plenty over there!" laughed the pixie-piper, pointing to a big pussy willow.

John looked. He could only see a

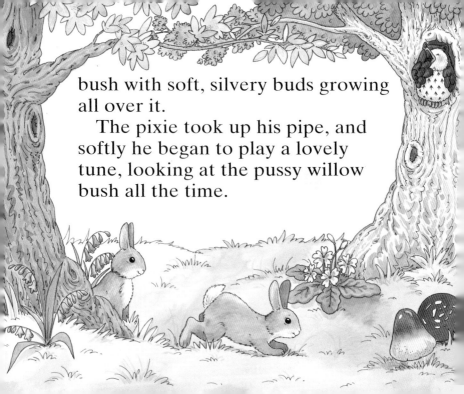

bush with soft, silvery buds growing
all over it.

The pixie took up his pipe, and
softly he began to play a lovely
tune, looking at the pussy willow
bush all the time.

John looked too, and he saw a wonderful sight – so wonderful he could hardly believe his eyes! For the silver pussy willow buds had

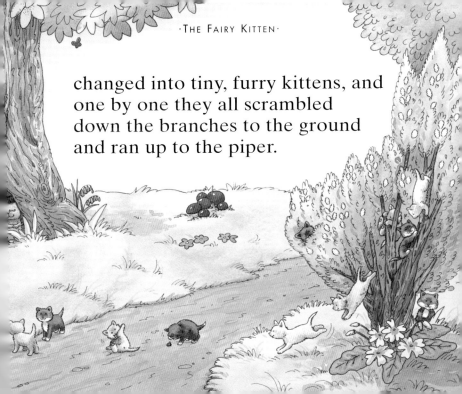

changed into tiny, furry kittens, and
one by one they all scrambled
down the branches to the ground
and ran up to the piper.

They danced and frisked round him, and ran after their little tails, for all the world like real kittens.

The piper stopped playing on his pipe.

"Now," he said, "you have to find your kitten. Which one is she? Quick! Can you see her? You must find her before they all go back to the tree and turn into pussy willow again!"

John ran after them,
and picked up a little
silvery kitten small enough
to fit into a nutshell!
He had found his kitty!

Then he watched the others climb up the branches and one by one turn into soft, silvery buds again!

The piper blew his pipe once more, and John's kitten grew bigger and bigger until it was just the right size.

"There you are!" said the pixie. "Don't tell anyone it's a fairy kitten. They won't believe you. Thank you for helping me, and I'm glad I've been able to help you in return. Goodbye."

He vanished, and left John alone with his fairy kitten. He ran home as fast as he could.

"Why, John!" cried his mother, "so you've found your kitty after all! I *am* glad!"

John told heaps of people how he found his fairy kitten – but the pixie was right, nobody believed him. Not even his best friend, Robert.

He didn't mind. He knew what nobody else did – and that was the place where fairy kittens come from!

And next time you see pussy willow, have a good look at it. I think you will say it's no wonder the fairies made kittens from such soft furry buds!